A Koala for Katie

An Adoption Story

Jonathan London

Illustrated by Cynthia Jabar

Albert Whitman & Company, Morton Grove, Illinois

To Louise, Frank, Sylvia and Madeline,
Marianne and Holly — who have lived
this story well. J.L.

For Anna. C.J.

3BERRYOO113978

Text © 1993 by Jonathan London.
Illustrations © 1993 by Cynthia Jabar.
Published in 1993 by Albert Whitman & Company,
6340 Oakton Street, Morton Grove, Illinois 60053.
Published simultaneously in Canada
by General Publishing, Limited, Toronto.
Printed in the U.S.A.
10   9   8   7   6   5   4   3   2   1

The text of this book is set in Stempel Schneidler.
The illustrations are rendered in ink, watercolor, and colored pencil.
Design by Lucy Smith.

Library of Congress Cataloging-in-Publication Data

London, Jonathan, 1947–
A Koala for Katie / Jonathan London : illustrated by Cynthia Jabar.
p.   cm.
Summary: On a trip to the zoo, Katie gets a special present that
helps her realize how much her adoptive parents love her.
ISBN 0-8075-4209-1
[1. Adoption–Fiction.   2. Parent and child—Fiction.]
I. Jabar, Cynthia, ill.   II. Title.
PZ7.L8432Ko   1993
[E]—dc20
93-16085
CIP
AC

A Note for Parents

As you struggle to talk to your child about adoption, it will help to recall what a common experience adoption is.

Taking responsibility for a child not born into one's family is a practice that has been going on for centuries, in many cultures. Today, in the United States, thousands of children are adopted every year. Many are adopted as infants, like Katie in this story. Some are adopted by stepparents following a death or divorce. Other children are older, even teenagers, when they come into their adoptive families. Children who cannot live with their birth parents are sometimes adopted by grandparents, other extended family members, or by their foster parents. Many children are from a race or culture different from their adoptive families. This adds new, enriching perspectives to a family's life.

Young children begin to learn about their own birth and adoption by asking questions. Answer your child honestly and in a matter-of-fact way, with simple information he or she can understand. Emphasize what your child shares in common with all other children. Explain that he or she grew inside a birth mother and had a birth father, just like everyone else. Reassure your child that you will be there to offer care and love, and to do all the things parents are supposed to do for their children.

Adoptive parents need to remember that being adopted is part of who their children are, and that they will wrestle with the fact of their adoption off and on throughout their lives. The ones who are most able to support them are their adoptive parents. You are the best person to reassure your child that he or she is accepted and valued — a cherished person, who brings to the family very special potential and gifts.

Norma Nelson
Northwest Adoption Exchange
Seattle, Washington

Katie thought a lot about babies.

Sometimes she pretended she was having one.

"Mommy?" said Katie one morning, "was I in my real mommy's belly?"

"Of course you were, Katie," Mommy said. "But I'm your real mommy, too."

"But I wasn't in *your* belly."

"No, sweetie. I can't have a baby, you know. That's why Daddy and I wanted *you* so very, very much."

After breakfast, Katie asked her mom,
"Why didn't my first mommy want me?"
"Remember what I told you?" Mommy said.
"She was too young to take good care of you.

"She loved you, Katie, and she wanted you
to have a better life than she could give you."

After lunch, Katie and her mom and dad
went to the zoo.
Katie stretched out her neck at the giraffes.

She waddled like a penguin with her dad.

Then they came to the place where a baby koala clung to her mama.

"Mommy, Daddy? Who would take care of that baby if her mommy couldn't anymore?" Katie asked.

"Well, if the baby's lucky," said her dad, "the zoo might find another mother for it."

"Wouldn't that be sad?" said Katie. "I mean, if that baby lost her mommy?"

"It would be," said her mom. "But the baby could be happy with a new mother, too."

"If the new mommy loved her, you mean?"

"Yes, honey. If the new mommy loved her the way Daddy and I love you."

Later, they went to the zoo shop. And then Katie saw it.

"Mommy, Daddy! Can I have that koala? Please, please!"

Katie's dad looked at Katie's mom.
Katie's mom smiled and said, "A
special gift for a special girl."

After supper, Katie played with her koala. "Mama Koala loved you," said Katie, "but she couldn't take care of you. So I'm your mommy now."

"I'm hungry!" said Baby Koala.

"Here are some yummy leaves," said Katie. "Eat up!"

Suddenly they heard something moving through the forest.

"I'm scared!" cried Baby Koala.

"Shush! Climb on my back!" said Katie.

A giant snake was coming. They could hear it sliding along the forest floor. Katie climbed up a tree, with Baby Koala clinging, clinging.

The snake wound round and round, pulling itself silently closer and closer. Katie stretched her striped pajamas over her head so she looked like a tiger, and growled. *Grrrrrr.*

The snake *hissssssssed,* flicked its forked tongue…and slithered off.

Baby Koala was safe!

"I'll protect you always," said Katie, giving her a big hug.

At bedtime, Mommy kissed the top of Katie's head. "I like your baby," she said.

"I'm really her mommy now," said Katie.

"And you're really our little girl," Daddy said, tucking Katie in.

"Goodnight, Mommy," said Baby Koala. "I'm glad you adopted me."

"Goodnight, Baby Koala," said Katie. "I'm glad, too."